THE URBAN EROTICA
FAIRY TALE COLLECTION

I0583739

Pinocchio
& the
Blow Up Doll

THE URBAN EROTICA
FAIRY TALE COLLECTION

Pinocchio
& the
Blow Up Doll

HONEY CUMMINGS

4 Horsemen
Publications, Inc.

4 Horsemen Publications, Inc.
1497 Main St. Suite 169
Dunedin, FL 34698
4horsemenpublications.com
info@4horsemenpublications.com

Cover & Typesetting by Battle Goddess Productions
Editior Vanessa Valiente

Ebook ISBN: 978-1-64450-192-4
Print ISBN: 978-1-64450-193-1

Dedication

For all my wonderful readers, here's a little Holiday Magic with a fairy tale spin!

Happy Holidays,

XOXO Honey Cummings

Words from the Author

I want to take this moment to thank all my readers. You've all been wonderfully supportive, and I love reading your reactions and reviews. These fantastical books are intended to be fun. For Fairy Tale Erotica Collection, I wanted them written more on the contemporary side by chasing missed opportunities and magical moments the readers secretly wish had unfolded. There's a hint of mischief that magically ends the story on a higher note. Life's funny like that at times!

As for the Urban Legend Collection, this is for all those shifter, paranormal, and fantasy lovers who dream of being swept away into a love story with someone who isn't quite from the same world. There's something thrilling about the not-so-human fantasy characters falling head over heels in love. Throughout the series, funny moments emerge, because for me, love has its share of awkward confessions. In the end, that's perfectly okay; in fact, it's normal!

This book was part of a giveaway earlier this year, a tradition I hope to bring back on an annual basis. It was a chance for fans to receive free books (though the pandemic has slowed the physical prizes from being sent out in a timely manner), and for one lucky fan to win the Grand Prize: naming a major character after them in this Holiday Special.

Congratulations to the
grand prize winner, Zelda!

Thank you to everyone who participated in my giveaway!

May you all stay safe during the holiday season!

1

Full Monty

No matter how hard Noc tried to avoid revealing his full name, it always came down to this moment—him standing there as everyone laughed so hard, they almost couldn't breathe.

Family naming traditions were a bitch.

This time he had managed to go almost a whole year at his now not-so-new job as "Noc." Besides, if Noc worked out for Noctis in Final Fantasy XV, how could he go wrong? That is, until the Secret Santa list had circulated the office this morning. Human Resources had listed his *full* name, and the staff came to life, assuming it was some kind of holiday gag.

Pinocchio Geppetto. Dammit, I go on vacation after today. Why now?

Noc didn't look like a pushover. He worked out on occasion, did parkour as a teen, while his mom had him play soccer for a number of years before that. He had decently sized biceps, a six-pack he tried to maintain, hazel eyes, and thick mid-length black hair. Thanks to his Italian heritage, he never lost his summer tan, a natural deep-toned olive skin that was famous among his relatives.

Dread pressed into him as he confessed to his supervisor, "It's not a gag. That's my *real* name. So, whoever draws Pinocchio, that's me. And I'd like to keep that quiet."

At his last job, he'd almost gotten away with using "Noc" and yet, it rose to the surface. Ultimately, the running gag of "knock on wood" jokes had sent him packing. He resigned and moved to a different city, landing a Lead Account Manager position. To offset a potential harassment suit, the company made him sign an agreement and gave him a hell of a severance. Naturally, he used it just to move elsewhere, to start again fresh. Making friends had been easier when no one knew his grand secret.

Thanks, mom. This is the worst name you can bestow a grown-ass man. Dammit, I'd love to change it legally, but I can't. She'd be heart broken. She takes pride in our Italian roots and the story inspired by our family generations ago. It was never meant in ill-intent...

"Let me get this straight, that's your *legal birth name?*" His supervisor struggled to get the words out as he chuckled. "How'd I miss this?"

Rolling his eyes, Noc ran a hand through his thick, black locks. "Everyone assumes it's a gag."

"Yeah, why wouldn't they? It's a storybook character's name." His supervisor continued to giggle as he marveled at the sheet . "What was your mother thinking?"

Noc met his gaze, stern and stoic. "She takes pride that our family inspired the legend."

His supervisor swallowed, stifling his laughter at the heated gaze. "R-right. That's... I didn't realize it was based on an actual legend."

"Well, it is." Noc at last sighed. *Now would be a perfect time to set boundaries. Don't repeat past mistakes here, Noc.* "Look, I left my last job because I was getting harassed by coworkers over this exact reason."

The supervisor cringed. "R-right. Didn't you say you left there with a hell of a severance over a situation?"

"Yeah. A situation just like this." Noc pointed at the paper. "I expect you to make it clear that I won't be bombarded by a billion puns and jokes about my name, Bob."

"Oh shit." Bob's eyebrows lifted high. "It got bad, then?"

"Trust me, it was rough." Noc glanced at his reflection, his hazel eyes piercing him in this tense moment. *I am so pissed, there's no hiding it this time. Is it ok to be this aggressive with my own supervisor? I mean, I suppose considering why I left my last job, I can't fret over the order*

4

of command over this. He needs to understand I am not playing around.

"Look, Noc. I'll keep this at a dull roar. If anyone starts up, let me know." Bob looked at the paper and laughed again. "I'm sorry. I mean, I'm sure it was cute as a kid but, damn dude. Why not get a name change or something?"

"I've thought about it, but it might send my mother to an early grave." He shook his head. "I mean, she's moved back to Italy to take care of my grandparents, so you can imagine the hell that will cause in the entire family if I dare to do that."

"Oh! Aren't you going to Italy for the holidays?" Bob changed topics, shoving the paper out of view.

"I was, but we didn't want to risk anyone else getting sick. This virus hasn't exactly dissipated. There's always Easter." Noc spun on his heel, heading for the door. "Thanks for understanding."

Noc quickly shut the door behind him, cutting off whatever Bob had wanted to say next. Inhaling deep, he scanned the cubicles with gatherings of giggling people lipping *Pinocchio*. His next mission was to confront Gina in Human Resources.

I went as far as filling out my paperwork under my alias. Only HR sensitive paperwork had my full name.

Gathering his nerves, he marched toward the administrative offices on the other side of the sales floor. Her door was open, so he pushed inside and slammed it closed behind him. Jolting, Gina dropped her pen and stared at him wide-eyed. After a few blinks, a wide grin grew on her face.

"We need to talk," Noc demanded.

Gina's cheeks flushed. "Yes? What's the matter?"

"You put my whole name on the Secret Santa list. I *explicitly* requested you not to. Besides, that isn't the name written on my paperwork," he said, getting straight to the point.

She rose to her feet and leaned over her desk. "But you have an adorable name."

Noc's eyes fell to the exposed cleavage under her unbuttoned shirt. His face heated, swallowing as he fought to bring his eyes back to hers. The rest of her attire seemed, unusual. A short skirt, her bright blue bra could be seen through the thin white blouse, and her lipstick darker. Even the eyeshadow screamed she had plans to go on a date.

I don't remember petite, curvy Gina being the type to dress so provocatively. Should I tell her a button came lose or did she do that on purpose? Is that a blue fairy tattoo on breast? Holy shit, Gina has ink!

Gina marched from behind her desk, forcing Noc to step back until his slammed against the door. She approached, hips swinging in her red stilettos until she could reach behind him.

Locking the door, her brown eyes looked him up and down.

He blinked. *Did she just take stock of me? This isn't a club, I mean, last time a girl checked me out like that we ended up fucking in a bathroom stall.*

Her body language was stranger, more seductive than normal, stirring something inside him. Noc opened his mouth to speak, but snapped his jaw closed. Gina winked, smiling wide as she started to shut the blinds that peered into the sea of cubicles. Noc tilted his head, curious what in the world was happening. His initial understanding seeming to be screaming he was about to hook up with his HR rep. Her skirt so short, he swore he could see her ass cheeks and hints of a... *blue thong to match?*

"Let me make it up to you, Noc," she offered, undoing a button, giving him a peek of her blue, lacy bra.

"Excuse me?" He shook his head in disbelief. *Did I just walk into an office themed porno? Where are the cameras? This can't be happening right now.* "Uh, Gina, I don't think that's the kind of..."

She had closed the gap between them, a finger pressing against his lips. "I didn't realize you had such an adorable name to match your cuteness, Pinocchio."

"Wait, what?" The weight of his situation started to unfold in his mind. *No, it couldn't be. Gina intentionally did this because...* "Let me get this straight, you did this on purpose?"

"Maybe?" She shrugged as she unhooked two more buttons on her white blouse, freeing her breasts completely. "You know, I'm a huge fan of those movies."

"Porn movies?" Noc's confusion tangled with the involuntary bulge in his pants. *Shit, she's got a big set of tits.*

Gina blushed, laughing as she finished unbuttoning her blouse, revealing a taut bra filled with soft flesh. "Heavens no." She motioned at a display high on the wall behind her desk, where she perched herself. "Disney movies."

"Oh." He cleared his throat, seeing the unusual amount of older film characters staring down at them. "Right. Those movies."

Wait, are those all Pinocchio themed characters? There's more Pinocchio's up there than I've even seen or been gifted in my lifetimes. Which means...

"So, what do you want first?" she offered, teasingly pulling her skirt higher, revealing her matching thongs.

Noc closed his eyes, sucking on his inner cheek as his logic and cock battled for decision-making rights. "Gina, I don't think this is a good idea. I mean, I'm flattered but technically we're still on the clock?"

I doubt that's gonna stop her.

"I can give you a blow job." Gina's voice deepened with provocative demand. "Or let you lick my pussy." <Insert an action from Noc.> "Or we can cut to the chase and let you bend me over the desk and hammer me."

Shit! She's out of her mind! He peeked at her, swallowing. "Gina, I just find my name

10

embarrassing and just wanted it..." With practiced skill, she reached back, and the bra came lose, pink nipples erect as the blue bra landed on the floor with the blouse. "...wanted... wanted... you have magnificent breasts." *Fuck! What am I saying!*

"Oh, you're a boob man, huh?" She excitedly jumped to her feet, making her breasts bounce in a way that tightened Noc's pants further.

She's really going to do this. We're really going to do this. When in Rome?

Wiggling out of her panties, only her black skirt and red stilettos remained. Her blonde, wavy hair bounced around her shoulders as she waltzed toward the exterior window. Bending over, she lifted the skirt to show off her pink folds, her pussy wet and ready for him. Noc's cock pressed tighter against his pants, the tingling arousal starting to drown out all reasoning in his mind. Gina pressed her breasts hard against the window and wiggled her ass as if invoking a bull to charge.

11

Being on the fifth floor, midday, I wonder if someone can see her from here. On that note, would they see me pounding her this far back with her breasts... fuck it, let's do this.

Noc rushed to unfasten his pants, taking one final look at the locked door and closed blinds. "We gotta be quiet. These walls are thin."

"You're assuming you can fuck me hard enough to make me squeal." She smacked her ass cheek hard, a hand-shaped welp already taking shape.

"This isn't exactly what I had in mind as part of my Christmas bonus..." he muttered, approaching with caution. "You get too loud, and it's over."

"Fuck me, Pinocchio."

He blinked, his cock throbbing at her weighted command. "Well, if I'm honest, this is the first anyone has used my full name."

"Fucking lie to me and fuck me with your hard wood," she moaned as her other hand slid between her thighs from the other way.

Noc's eyes fell to where her fingers rubbed across her wet pussy. They dipped between the swollen folds, thrusting a few times before pulling back wet. He bit his lip, stroking his hard cock. Retreating to her clit, her finger circled slow and she moaned once more. He took a step forward, but again hesitated.

Man, this will complicate things...

"Lie to me."

"Excuse me?" He took a nerve-wracking step forward again, heart racing and arousal growing. "You want me to do what now?"

"Fucking lie to me, Pinocchio," her voice deepened with desire.

"I'd be lying if I thought this was a good idea." He half laughed and caught her reflection in the window. *Shit, she's fucking serious.* "I've been dreaming about you, Gina?"

"You lie." She smirked, wild and sinister. "Again."

"I've always wanted to fuck you?" he offered.

"Fucking liar... tell me *more*, make that dick grow for me, baby." Gina seemed hot and bothered by his clueless attempts.

"I only took this job to fuck you?"

"Liar." She wiggled, her pussy dripping. "Look how long your wood is getting. Fuck me with your lies, Pinocchio! Fuck me with your growing wood!"

Noc came closer, his thick, hardened length rubbing along her opening.

"Oh, it's nice and hard."

His hands caressed her tight ass cheeks, gliding up until he could grip her hips under the raised skirt. "Here's another lie, *I have a condom.*"

Wonder if she thought about that little fact.

2

The Paperwork

Noc locked eyes with her reflection as his cock rubbed against her swollen folds. Silky and hot, he throbbed with the desire to shove inside her wet heat. The way her back arched so that her breasts were pressed firmly against the glass made him jealous. There was no way someone in the parking lot couldn't see those headlights, but she was really into this moment.

I'd rather rub my cock between them. Or better yet, catch one of those cotton candy pink nipples in my teeth for fun. Granted, this is kind of hot.

"Don't you worry, Noc. I plan on swallowing."

He didn't need any more goading. He shoved hard and fast inside her. She bit her lip to stifle her yelp. Her cheek pressed hard against the glass now as he thrusted into her with hard, long strokes. Noc could feel Gina tighten around his cock. She began panting, hands and arms bracing her on the glass. Her legs shook. Noc leaned forward, the building friction of her tight pussy intoxicating. He landed a palm flat on the glass above her, rocking back slow and slamming forward fast. Each time her yelp grew louder.

Dammit, I'm losing it. This is a little unnerving even for me.

Closing his eyes, he imagined someone he wanted more. He agonized on the edge of peaking. His imagination sought out a blonde, elven vixen. Something surreal, something otherworldly seemed more realistic than this unfolding moment between him and his human resource officer. Noc let his mind take him to a moment of licking a breast, having such a noble being kneel before him. IN his mind, he moaned the name of a game character he had crushed one for all his life.

Zelda.

A moan escaped Gina, her hands covering her mouth as she pulsed and gushed. He had grown harder in the moments of gamer boy fantasies. Her orgasm exploded, and he slowed to watch chills roll over her skin like ripples on a lake. Despite it, she was warm and soft under his grip. The pulsing of her pussy on his rock-hard cock tipped him dangerously close to peaking.

"I'm coming..." he huffed, pulling out.

Spinning on her heels, Gina's lips wrapped around his cock. Noc's other palm thudded on the glass, his legs turning to jelly as she didn't let him lose any ground on his overwhelming ecstasy. The bopping waves thrusted to and fro as she sucked on his shaft. Her tongue wiggled against his underbelly. At last, the tip pressed down the back of her throat and he groaned.

What's the etiquette of grabbing HR by the hair to hold a deep throat? Shit...

A hand fisted against the glass, eyes shut tight as he fought the urge to hold her there for a moment longer. He came, *hard.* She swallowed and suckled and brought on another spurt, then a third. Satisfied, he sighed as she slid off his cock with a pop. She ran her tongue from the base to tip one last time, making him grunt. At last he opened his eyes, backing away to give her space to stand.

"It's a shame I'm not free this weekend." She shrugged and brushed pass him. "I wouldn't mind trying to straddle and ride your wood one more time, Pinocchio." Circling around her desk, she plucked her bra and shirt off the floor as she continued, "I'm sorry to expose you twice today." She winked, pulling her bra back on. "But in all fairness, I'm your Secret Santa. I rigged it, and you were mine"

"Well," Noc tucked himself away, glancing at the marks of Gina's breasts, face, and hands on the window, "that's gotta be the strangest Secret Santa gift I've ever received."

She giggled. "No, silly. That was just me wanting to have my way with someone named after my all-time favorite character. I mean, don't get me wrong, you're super-hot, Noc. A real nice guy, but finding out your real name..." She paused, face blushing. "All reasonable thoughts just ceased. Don't you dare say anything about this. Anyway, your gift is in that sealed box in the chair, but wait until tonight before you open it."

Noc turned to see a rather big box wrapped up and a huge bow tied on it. "Why wait until tonight?"

Gina smiled, arching her eyebrows high as she buttoned her blouse with impeccable speed. "You can say I hope you think of me tonight."

Oh shit. This can't be good.

"Noc, look, I am off for the rest of the holiday week too. Thank you for starting my vacation off with a bang." She picked her panties up, then shoved them into her purse. "I'm spending the whole week with Mr. Townsend."

Noc paled, eyes wide. "Wait, my supervisor? B-bob?"

"Oh? Huh, I didn't realize you worked under him." She paused, typing on her computer. "You know, let me do this much for you, how about a promotion? I would love to see more of you and a managerial role would make that possible."

"Gina, Bob's married." Noc sucked on his cheek. "And her name's Mary."

"Yeah, I know." She hit enter and turned to dig in one of her desk drawers. "But you see, every holiday they spend it with... someone else. It's some kind of swinger's arrangement. In the end, I literally get to have a good time in some fancy resort in Miami for the week. I hate going home for the holidays to see my family. They're in Ohio and the snow is *ugh*." She pulled out paper towels and a bottle of window cleaner. "Look, I'll clean up in here, so you can leave early and get paid for the whole day."

"Then who is Mary spending the week with? I know they don't have kids but…" Noc's curiosity got the best of him as he pried further into this weird dynamic unfolding within his workplace. *Exactly how many people in this damn building are fucking each other?*

"You know Heather in sales?" The sway of her hips made his eyes follow her to the window. "In fact, it's the third holiday they'll be spending together."

"Heather?" He tilted his head. "The same Heather who can beat any man in this building at an arm-wrestling contest? The Gina Carano could be her twin, Heather? But Mary is so tiny and frail, even next to you."

"Yes, that Heather. The big, beautiful gal with her tall, black boots, torn jeans, white camis, and plaid shirts." Gina paused a moment, then wiped breast print from the window. "Now that I'm thinking about it, I bet she's a Nirvana fan."

"How many in the office know about... this?" Noc's brow folded, his mind racing. *What planet did I wake on this morning?*

Gina snorted. "Like the whole office. I mean, Mary and Bob have already made their rounds and don't be shocked if she doesn't offer you a ride in her office next."

"Wait, what?" Noc covered his mouth, his imagination seeing sweet little Mary coaxing him in and shoving the financial reports off her desk. "No, I couldn't..."

"Oh she's a good time, though careful, she gets rough." Stretching on her tiptoes, she sprayed the window and wiped the area one last time where his palm marks had been.

"Rough?" he marveled. "Exactly... what the hell does that mean?"

"Oh? You really don't know about all this?" Turning back to him, she gave him a skeptical look. "How long have you been here?"

"Eleven months," he replied flatly. *Shouldn't HR know that?*

"Ah, well." She returned to her desk, dropping the cleaner into a drawer, then kicking it closed. "My adorable, oh-so-innocent Pinocchio, should be aware she's really, *really,* into BDSM."

Noc's eyes nearly crossed as he imagined tiny Mary in a black negligée, perfectly fitted for a dominatrix featured on PornHub.com. Glancing at the present wrapped with ribbons and bows, he sighed. Again, his mind cooked up what the mystery item could possibly be with all the new, naughty dirt he had gained about his fellow coworkers. *Shit, my bosses. Every supervisor in this joint has some underground sex ring happening, what the fuck is up with that?*

Shaking the images from his head, he turned back to Gina who seemed to be settling back in to... *work?*

"Um, ok, well thank for..." He picked up the rather weighty gift. "This. Um, yeah, heading home and gonna start my holiday week a tad early."

"Oh?" She smiled, her eyes never leaving the screen as she tapped away on her keyboard. "Well, just remember...think of me when you open it and play with your new *toy*."

Noc inhaled deep. "R-right," he said as he opened the door and dove into the sales floor.

At least no one has seemed to notice our little hookup, but damn... What the hell is going on in this place? They did, they had to have heard that last shriek. Maybe this is normal for them, which would explain why they aren't phased. Have I just been accepted into some weird, secret sex club?

From her open office door, Mary locked eyes with him and winked. Then he stumbled as he watched Heather lean into Mary's ear whispering or... *did she just openly lick her earlobe?*

It was more than enough to turn him for the door and elevator.

I got my car keys, my wallet, fuck my jacket. I'll brave the cold just to get out from under all this... heat.

3

Secret Santa

Noc couldn't shake the nagging sensation lingering in his trunk. Outside, the temperature plunged as another cold front advanced just as the sun began to set over the bustling cityscape. He had left it there, came home and ordered out in hopes he would just leave it there until he found a dumpster big enough to toss it in. The phone buzzed, his order left at the door and he waited. Thanks to the pandemic, his holiday plans were cancelled including his plan B to hit the local bar. Flights back to see his mother in Italy were impossible now with the airport shutting down and freezing ticket sales.

Guess if I even wanted to brave it out there wearing a mask, it's just not meant to happen.

Grabbing his bagged dinner off the stoop, he returned to the kitchen counter. As he opened the containers, a blast of pad Thai and pork dumplings sent his stomach rumbling. He had missed lunch altogether thanks to the event with Gina. His mind wondered back to what unfolded in her office. Shoveling the food faster, he was back to seeing the damned box.

Well, maybe I should at least see what the fuck was so heavy? I mean, it a good-sized box.

Chucking the empty containers into the trash, he snatched the keys off the counter. He muttered curses under his breath as he braved the night air. Snow began to fall as he removed the box from the truck, then rushed into his townhome.

Setting it on the couch, he waited a moment, mind racing with possibilities it held. *Don't tell me Gina bought a sex swing...something for us to use together. I mean, it's big and heavy. How did that tiny blond even get this thing into the office.*

"Fuck it..."

He pulled at the bow, failing to unloosen it. At last, he scoured his kitchen drawers for a knife and at sliced the ribbons away. The wrapping paper ripped away easy enough, but the bare cardboard box underneath gave nothing away about what may be inside. Scoffing, he slid the knife over the packing tape and forced it open. Opening the flaps wide, he took a step back.

No, I think this is the worst idea ever...

Noc covered his mouth, knotting his brow. Blinking, he took in the folded form. Frayed blonde hair, flesh colored skin, red lips stuck in a permanent "oh" as she stared up in helpless blue eyes. The sex doll was deflated and between her flattened breasts was a note. Noc cringed. The implications of a doll for her man-doll sending a shiver up his spine.

> *My beloved Pinocchio,*
>
> *Please think of me when you play with her.*

Your friendly neighborhood HR,

Gina <3

"Really. Of all the..." Groaning, he crumbled up the note, closing his eyes against the blinding, red anger. "Because...my name's Pinocchio. It doesn't mean I have a doll fetish, lady." Peeking open one eye, he looked down at the crumbled plastic being. "Well, let's at least blow you up and get a better idea what exactly I'm dealing with. I don't think I've seen one of these in person."

He peeled the doll out of the box, then unfolded it. This wasn't a simply cheesy gag gift vinyl made blow up doll. Gina had found something well over the twenty-dollar limit they had set for the rest of the office. The rubber was soft and fleshy to the touch, not as wrinkly as he'd expect her legs and arms to be as they unraveled.

Damn, this is a high-end doll made to be used in all seriousness.

Glancing over the front, his eyes glided over the nipples, down the torso and lingered on the pink slot meant to be her pussy. Swallowing he flipped her over, perplexed there was a slot for anal too. *No fun opening missed I see.* As he searched upward, relief washed over him as he located the valve in the middle of her back.

"Oh man. I was so worried this would be a nipple or worse, in her ass like a bad joke."

Steeling himself, he drew in a large breath and began to blow air into the doll. He watched with each round as her limbs stiffened and soon her torso began making the process difficult. Fumbling with her, breast still not fully inflated as he tried to find some means to hold the naked inanimate woman, he found himself pursing lips against the small of her back.

So...this is awkward.

A hand gripped a breast and he left it there in defeat. After a few more rounds of air, he started to feel lightheaded. The groping of her breast became firmer, more realistic until he reached the point where the air wouldn't go

29

further in without pushing back into his mouth. Using the tip of his tongue to plug the hole, he managed to push the plug in with his hand, then popped it inward to smooth her back.

Breathing in and out, regaining the oxygen he had given her, he stood up and placed her on the couch. She lay stiffly across the furniture, looking surprised to be propped up so haphazardly. Noc crossed his arms, his brow lowering as he observed the inanimate sexual partner he had been gifted. She seemed as nervous and shocked as he did. Without the deflated, squashed look, she curved a little more naturally than he had expected. The straight locks of hair waterfalled all around her like a princess.

Am I really thinking she's hot...? I need a shower. Maybe on the cold side.

Noc's heart raced, his face heating from his rising emotions.

I mean, it seemed like a cheesy mockup, but after filling her out with some hot air...

He stripped down, tossing his clothes all over the bedroom floor as he beelined for the bathroom. Living alone had its advantages, one he had frequently enjoyed while strutting around the apartment completely naked. Setting his phone up to play music, he tilted his head as a ninety's throwback by Santana came on and he left it. The knobs squeaked and icy water rained down on him.

I still feel dirty after my rendezvous with HR, regretting not doing this first.

Gina's perfume seemed to still linger for a moment until he at last reached for the body soap. His entire day seemed surreal. The idea his real name had been exposed to coworkers once again made the muscles in his back tense. He reached for the shampoo and conditioner, scrubbing his hair in frustration. Unlike the last job, this powder keg took an unexpected turn.

Shit, I shouldn't have slept with Gina. She's my human resource officer! "What the hell was I thinking?"

Shampoo slipped into his eyes, stinging. Murmuring profanities, he rushed to rinse it all off. Despite clearing it from his hair and face, his eyes still stung, and he closed them tight. Turning the shower off, he went scrambling for the towel. His hand gripped the empty towel rack. Grumbling more curses, he blindly moved toward the door. As he reached for the doorknob, a towel met his hand. He gripped it and started drying his hair and face, eyes still stinging.

Did I leave it hanging on the bathroom door? That's weird...

"Is that what you were looking for?" The female voice made him drop the towel and take a step back.

"Who the fuck..." Blinking out the last of the soap, he stared wide-eyed.

Before him stood a completely naked blonde with curvy hips and large breasts. She blushed, batting her eyes at him. Unlike Gina, her blonde hair was long and fell in straight locks like a waterfall around her breasts. Pink nipples stood erect and his eyes chased the contours of her body, the way her shaven pussy tucked between thick thighs making him aroused. He covered his cock with his hands, the muscles in his torso tightening with alarm.

"Who are you?" He snapped his eyes to the blue irises glowing with magic.

"I... well, you haven't given me a name yet." She frowned, cupping his cheek with her hand. "But thank you for blowing me up earlier."

Noc's mind raced, thoughts grinding into one another as if gears locking up. "Blew you... up?"

Disbelief hit him, he walked pass her and marched into his living room. The box still laid in tatters and he examined it, smelling it, and shaking it as if some unforeseen chemical leaked from it. Scanning the room, the sex doll he had blown up moments before was nowhere to be seen. He covered his mouth, turning back to the bedroom door where the naked woman stood and smiled sweetly when their gazes met. She didn't seem to be unnerved being in a stranger's apartment, completely naked along with him, and it sent chills down Noc's spine. Standing before him was a real-life version of the doll.

She looks like the doll. Same height, features, breast size. There's something so unnatural about this. It's gotta be acid, or LSD, or...

"What the hell did Gina lace on that damn doll." He started pacing the room, holding his head. "She's my HR officer. She knows where I live. And now...I'm hallucinating on some unknown drug she clearly laced her *gift*." Spinning on his heels, he rushed the front door to flip all the locks, drawing the chain he never used into place.

What if she's already here? Fuck.

Ignoring the completely naked woman in his home, he checked the rest of the house, while his paranoia wondered if Gina had snuck in during his shower. As he continued to inspect his closet and under his bed, he couldn't help stealing glances of the gorgeous blonde. Again, he could feel himself aroused taking in the peachy tone of her skin, the soft pink of her nipples, and the way her lips unfolded like flower petals.

She looked so much like a real life... *a name, she said she...*

"You're seriously waiting on me to name you?" he murmured, as he closed his closet. *Well, it doesn't seem my hallucination is going to fade any time soon. Might as well entertain this idea.*

"Oh yes, I really should have one, don't you think?" She took a step closer to him, clapping her hands with excitement. "Name me anything you'd like, the sexier the better."

"A sexy name..." He sashayed back to the other side of his room until the bed made a barrier between them. "I mean, you're just a fragment of my imagination or high." He reassured himself. "And I'm pretty sure Gina has something to do with all this..."

She titled her head. "Is that my name? Gina?" she asked, a sense of innocence in her voice.

"NONONONO!" He threw out his hands in panic. "*Hell* no."

"Then what do you want my name to be, Pinocchio?" She sat on his bed; her hands clasped on her plump thighs making his cock throb.

"Noc. Please, call me Noc," he said flatly.

"Noc, the Blue Fairy has blessed you with the perfect match. But please, I need a name."

Of course, why hadn't I considered that old story into the mix. Perhaps the Blue Fairy will answer my longtime wish and join us in a threesome I'll never forget.

"Zelda," he said firmly. "Your name is Zelda."

"I like Zelda." Her hands covered her heart, a look of relief on her face. "Thank you, Noc."

"Uh, you're welcome?" He shook his head. "Look, Zelda. I'm going to bed now."

"Wait, I wanted to..."

Noc threw up a hand to silence her. "It's been a long day and well, I think if I can just sleep this off, whatever this is," he motioned to her and himself a few times, "I might wake up a little less freaked out."

"Oh, I had no idea." She cupped her face. "And feeling so tired, you still took the time to inflate me."

"R-right." He flipped back his comforter. "Um, well, goodnight?" he offered.

She flipped her side of the comforter. "Get some rest, Noc."

"What are you doing?" he asked, his words rushed.

"Going to bed with you." As she crawled into bed, his heart fluttered catching a view of her pussy, prompting him to blush. "I'm cold and want to keep you company."

Noc narrowed his eyes. "F-fine, but I mean it. I'm going to sleep."

She's just a figment of my imagination, why the fuck am I getting all worked up over this?

4

Between the Sheets

The heat of fingers slid up his inner thigh, stirring him awake from a deep, deep slumber. He had fallen asleep faster than expected, even with a strange, naked woman snuggled in the curve of his arm, her soft skin and warm body instantly lulled him away.

Granted, he wasn't completely convinced he was riding on some mystery drug trance. Between the "meeting" with Gina and her *generous* gifts, he imagined he was snuggling with a sex doll in bed like some poor, drunk college student.

As the haze of sleep melted away, his mind shifted into erotic thoughts about *Zelda*.

Strangely, this version didn't have elven ears. His cock hardened as fingers began stroking his shaft. A moan escaped him; his eyes still closed. The tingling heat buzzed across his entire being as his pleasure increased.

A hot breath blew across the tip and his dick jumped in the grip.

Her fingers tightened around his shaft; the stroking grew firmer, more confident with every touch. A tongue slowly circled the tip of his cock. He hardened further, tilting his hips wanting more of the wet heat and its velvety texture. The tongue glided down and up his shaft, the hot pants promising against dick teased how close lips lay in the vagueness between the sheets. He gripped the sheets, still fighting sleep as his dreams took an erotic turned.

"Zelda," her name fell from his lips with unfiltered, provocative desire.

Lips slipped over the cap of his cock, and he moaned, angling so he could dip further into the slick mouth. A whimper escaped the mouth, and he became very aware his dream was not so imaginative. Eyes popping open, he saw a form covered in his blanket, someone had slipped between his legs. His knees pressed against a hot, soft body. The pleasure fogged his mind, unwilling to push them away as the bopped up and down his dick. He threw back the covers, the sultry blonde gobbling the entire length of his cock, suckling as she went. Breast swayed with her efforts, nipples teasing his thighs.

He inhaled swift. "Zelda," he said more firmly.

Their gazes locked and she pushed further down on his cock. The tip of his dick hit the back of her throat, and he grunted. She kept him there, suckling and wiggling her tongue against his throbbing hardened length as he teetered on the edge of an orgasm.

"Zelda," he breathed, body tensing as he fought the urge to come.

Slow and agonizing, she pulled back off his hardened length, her eyes on his until her lips broke away. "Yes, Noc?"

"You're still here?" he marveled, his mind failing to comprehend the weight of the reality and glancing at the clock. *It's been over six hours and...*

"Of course, I am." She sat up, her body gorgeous between his legs. He hissed as she arched upward into the right angle to present her breasts to him. "I'm yours, and *only* yours."

"R-right." Noc's heart pounded in his ears. "I thought, well." *What am I trying to say?* "I didn't think you were... *real*."

"Oh?" Zelda smiled, crawling atop him, her breast soft as they brushed against his torso. "What will it take to make it clear to you that I'm very real, a real-life woman meant only for you. I'm not going anywhere unless you send me away. I'm a real woman on every level, Noc."

"I mean, doesn't it normally start with a wish?" Noc smirked as her thighs pressed on side of his hips. "I don't recall making one, to tur a doll into a real––*live* woman."

"No, you didn't. It's not always prompted by the receiver. Sometimes, the Blue Fairy rewards

41

those who have worked hard or have failed to take time to find companionship with someone special." Zelda leaned in, her lips tickling his ear as she whispered, "In your case, you are given someone special when the perfect opportunity presented itself–– when you were gifted with me today."

Whispering into her ear, he challenged, "Even if it means turning a sex doll into a person? A little inappropriate for the Blue Fairy I would think."

"A doll is a doll." She kissed his neck and he shuddered. "But...would you rather me be a fragile, porcelain princess, Noc? Or someone... less anatomically correct?"

"Are you implying," he paused, inhaling her familiar, intoxicating, flowery scent before he dared to finish the sentence, "...that you were built to fuck me?"

She grinded her wet pussy against his hardened length. "You did blow me up, Noc. Now I can return the favor and blow *you*."

"That I did." He held his breath as the grinding sent shivers through him. "I just didn't think magic worked like this... and exchange of blowing one another."

"Touch me, grope my breast." She jerked his hand from his side, his palm cupping the soft flesh forcibly. "Touch me like you did when breathing life into me, Noc. I want to feel you kissing down my back once more, your breath against my skin like it's the first time all over again."

Noc shifted his hips, his cock sliding between her slick folds. Her pussy tightened as he rode, slow and deep. She tried to sit up, but he wrapped his arms around her, pulling her into him as he rocked back and forth, making her moan. His tongue lashed out, sliding across a nipple and her breath caught. Sucking the flesh between his lips, his appetite for her growing with each thrust. Every long suckle of her nipple rewarded him with the tightening of her pussy around his cock.

"Oh, Noc," she moaned his name, rocking her hips to deepen his penetration. "Noc, don't stop."

He switched breasts, enjoying the soft pillow of flesh. His hands wondered down the small of her back. One hand slid beyond the other until he could grip her ass. Her legs shook with her rising bliss. He sped up his thrusting, his lips releasing her breast so he could look up to see her face. Zelda arched her back, palms pressing down on his chest so she could shift once more to let him fuck her more deeply. He hardened under the heat of her hands.

"Noc, I'm..." her words failed her, his hands sliding over her body to hold her hips in place. "I think I'm..."

"I can tell..." he panted, trying to not lose the pacing and motion. "Come for me, Zelda."

"Y-yes." Her fingers dug into his chest as her pussy tightened on his thrusting cock.

"Give it to me, I want to watch you come for me," he confessed.

Sweat trickled down his temple, he suppressed his own orgasm, his groin aching for release. Zelda gasped. At last, an ecstasy filled cries escaped her, body arching as her orgasm started to edge closer. Her breasts bounced with each entry of his cock. His thighs were wet, her body gushing to receive him over and over again. Her panting and closed eyes left him wanting to see her blue irises. She was so tight, so close to peaking as her muscles tightened throughout her body.

"Look at me," he demanded.

Under heavy lidded eyes, her glowing, blue eyes peered down at him. "Don't stop," she begged.

"I'm so close," he muttered, slowing down. "I want to come with you but..."

"Fill me," she pleaded, grinding against him to regain the lost momentum. "Come with me."

"But..." he swallowed, the wet friction making his cock throb inside her. "...what if... if I cum inside you can't you..."

"I'm a fuck doll, Noc. FUCK ME!" She gripped his wrists, moving him off her hips, then shoving his hands onto her breasts. "Fuck me and fill me. I am yours! I want to come with you!"

Squeezing her breast hard, her pussy tightened as she continued bouncing atop him. He returned to the rapid, deep thrusting. She shrieked, her pussy squeezing his rock-hard cock and he lost his fight. He moaned and she screamed. He released her breasts and pulled her back down into him, pushing hard into her as he filled her with his cum. Her fingers clawed at the sheets, and he kept thrusting to make their orgasms linger until exhaustion claimed him. His heart beating fast and hard.

I've never had a moment this incredible with someone... holy hell...

After a moment, he released her, allowing her to roll off him. They panted, sweaty from the energy spent in the heat of passion. Noc slowly turned to face her, watching as she continued to ride the buzz of ecstasy. One of her hands gripped a breast, the other gliding down between her thighs. He watched her as he caught his breath, curious as she began pleasuring herself.

At last, he rolled to his side, propping his head up with an arm to get a better view.

Her eyes were shut tight, arching as she twisted a nipple. Following the length of her arm, he at last stopped where a finger circled over a swollen clit. Her fingers dipped inside her swollen lips often, drawing the wetness across the flesh to fuel her play. And then, she released a muffled moan.

"Are you using my cum to masturbate?" Noc sucked on his cheek, jealous and turned on by the notion.

"You felt so good..." she cooed, not slowing her work. "I just want to keep it going, just a little longer."

Shit, and I'm spent for a while. Dammit, I 'm aching to go again.

"Don't stop," she huffed, fingers dipping and thrusting in and out of her pussy.

47

He furrowed his brow. "Don't stop?"

"Don't stop watching me, Noc." The wanton want in her voice made him shiver in excitement.

Her brow furrowed, struggling to release a second orgasm. He ran a hand across her stomach, and she moaned. Her body twitched. A smirk crossed his face, trailing fingers over her arm, down her hip and over her thigh. He squeezed and rubbed Zelda's inner thigh, daring to knock knuckles with her working hand.

Is it wrong for me to embrace this fantasy, to be with Zelda? To taste and make love to her until I wake up from whatever dream, or high, I'm on...

5

Taste of Honey

When her legs began to shake, he knew she was drawing close to peaking once more. His refractory period would be a while, but he wanted to explore her body more. Leaning closer to her, he began suckling on her ear. His hand pulled her thigh against him and his cock. Licking and kissing, he was slow to taste her salty sweet taste.

She tilted her head to give him access. "So close," she breathed, encouraging him.

His hand slid higher, her fingers retreating to circling her clit. Fingers slipped inside her and she whimpered. Burning kisses continued down her collarbone, he worked his way back to suckling her breast. Her pussy tightened around his fingers and he began stroking, enjoying how she began him helping her get off. Her hips shifted, helping her grind against his hand. The shaking in her legs increased, visibly fighting the urge to clamp close in fear of stopping the pleasure he brought her.

"Feels so good," she moaned.

Abandoning her circling she gripped onto his wrought iron headboard. It goaded Noc to change tactics and he pulled away. She panted, breasts rising and falling in the faint light spilling across them from his open bathroom door. Forcing her legs open, he positioned his body between her knees. Bowing before her, his hazel gaze watched as her blue eyes widened with wonder. Running his tongue flatly across her opening sent her in a squeal of delight.

I suppose this means I'll be the first to taste her... and that's a rare treat.

Her clit was swollen, the pink pearl erect, easy to circle and flick with the tip of his tongue. Knees dug into his torso as a shiver rattled her entire body like an electrical shock running through her veins. His fingers slid back into her, stroking faster than before. Arching, she allowed him better access and he couldn't resist to take advantage.

Enjoying the jolts and jerks, he explored her pussy further. Giving her clit a break, his tongue teased her opening. She inhaled, holding her breath. He licked inside her, thrusting his velvety tongue in and out of her. Her moaning betrayed her, and he reached up to rub her clit once more using his thumb. Honey dripped as her body desired to keep him there.

He grew aggressive, making love to her in hunger as his tongue wiggled in her wet heat, unraveling her. The cries of passion escaping her drove something animalistic in him. He wanted to make her come. Wrapping his lips around her clit once more, he sucked and stroked inside her with his fingers.

"YES!" The visceral exclamation didn't make him slow, teeth teasing and fingers rubbing a new side in response. "OH! OH! FUCK YES!"

Zelda's orgasm peaked, her throbbing pussy gushing around his stroking fingers. Noc could care less about the wet sheets, wanting to see her body react to him more. His cock had begun to harden, and he towered over her, pushing his cock inside her. Groaning, he grinded in and out of her as she wailed. Hands released the headboard, clawing at his back as if desperate to keep him there. Moaning, the fire she invoked only made him grind harder, deeper.

I love how she touches my cock when she orgasms. I want to keep her going...

The way his torso waved against her, breasts keeping them tantalizingly close and apart all at once. Her screams faded into moans as she continued to cling to him, her knees rising to improve their connection. His arms flexed under his own weight, unwilling to stop looking at her face.

"I'm coming again..." she confessed.

"Then look at me," he beseeched, grunting as she tightened around his cock.

Noc's breath caught, mesmerized by her bright, blue irises glowing with a magic as he slowed each movement.

"Beautiful..." he searched her face. "Are you really mine and mine only?"

"Forever yours." She pulled him closer, locking lips.

Noc kissed her, hungry and passionate. He moaned as he began to peak, her tongue slipping into his own mouth wrestling for real estate in a fit of desire. To go this far and kiss for the first time. He pushed hard against her, releasing as she tightened. His arms dove under her, pulling her into him as they continued to kiss passionately. They rolled and he found himself under Zelda. Breaking their kiss, she sat up, straddling his waist. He grunted as she tightened on him.

As the orgasm dissipated, Noc could feel how exhausted his entire body had become, how every aching muscle begged for proper rest. He had never gone this hard and long with someone, but somehow, his inability to maintain the stamina pained him.

"Unfortunately, I'm spent," he relented.

"Oh no," she scrambled off him, his cock losing its stiffness. "You're deflating! Sh-should I blow you up?"

Her hands scoured his body, tickling him as she searched for his valve.

"No!" He grabbed her hands and pulled her back beside him. "How about you and I get some rest, and we'll give this a proper second round. Maybe try this out in a hot shower?"

Spooning her, he pulled the covers up. He nuzzled her neck, enjoying her natural, flowery scent.

"You can do this bathing?" she marveled.

He laughed. "Zelda, as long as you're willing, we'll try it in every humanly way possible."

"That sounds wonderful." She held his arms into her.

He started to doze off, but his anxiety kept him awake. His mind raced, and his earlier suspicions resurfaced, his beating heart haunting him.

At last, he forced himself to whisper his greatest fear. "Will you still be here when I wake up?" He swallowed, waiting for the reply.

"Of course," she replied, patting his hair.

"But will you still be..." he choked on the question and at last, pushed out the rest. "...still be you and not a... sex doll."

She sighed. "I will be whichever you prefer me to be."

His heart fluttered at the answer. "Then you stay as you are, no matter what."

"I'd like that very much, Noc." She laughed. "The Blue Fairy will be very pleased."

Another moment of silence lingered and at last, he thought to ask, "Who is the Blue Fairy?"

"Well, some people know her as Gina," replied Zelda. "Once she returns from vacation, she said she'll join us for a threesome."

Noc paled. "Join us?"

Pinocchio and the Blow Up Doll

Son of a... I guess it's true.
Be careful what you wish for.
THE END

Honey Cummings

A passionate, award-winning author of Fantasy, Honey has turned her aim towards erotica. Blending everyday scenarios and crafting them into steamy, blood-boiling moments for every shade of audience. Whether you want something short and hot like a student-teacher hook up to the more paranormal flair where Sleep with Sasquatch has unexpected bonus, look forward to erotic short stories, novellas, and hopefully a Trilogy in the future. Honey's debut erotic short landed No. 3 in Urban Erotica and continues to satisfy readers time and time again. Be sure to leave her a review and let her know what you think!

Pinocchio and the Blow Up Doll

https://www.amazon.com/Honey-Cummings/e/
B07WFX5FDX

www.AuthorHoneyCummings.com

instagram.com/authorhoneycummings

twitter.com/HoneyCummings2

facebook.com/
Author-Honey-Cummings-101408818012749

4HORSEMENPUBLICATIONS.COM

www.ingramcontent.com/pod-product-compliance
Lightning Source LLC
Chambersburg PA
CBHW020347110726
47898CB00003B/1067